LIFE WORKS!

DON'T SWEAT IT

HOW TO NAVIGATE BIG EMOTIONS

by Sloane Hughes

BEARPORT PUBLISHING

Minneapolis, Minnesota

Credits: Cover background, © cammep/Shutterstock; cover 1, 4–5, 8–9, 11, 13, 15–17, 19–20, 22–23 (monsters), © world of vector/Shutterstock; 2–3, 12–19, 24 (background), © fishStok/Shutterstock; 4 (sad), © ANURAK PONGPATIMET/Shutterstock, (happy), © Luis Molinero/Shutterstock; 5 (angry), © Firma V/Shutterstock, 5, Krakenimages.com/Shutterstock; 7, © Prostock-Studio/Shutterstock; 8, © Shift Drive/Shutterstock; 13, © Tatyana Vyc/Shutterstock; 15, © wavebreakmedia/Shutterstock; 16T, © fizkes/Shutterstock; 16B, © Gorodenkoff/Shutterstock; 17, © Monkey Business Images/Shutterstock; 19, © Coco Ratta/Shutterstock; 20-1, © Prostock-studio/Shutterstock, 20-2, © AJP/Shutterstock, 20-3, © PRESSLAB/Shutterstock, 20-4, © MNStudio/Shutterstock; 20-21, © Master1305/Shutterstock.

Library of Congress Cataloging-in-Publication Data

Names: Hughes, Sloane, author.
Title: Don't sweat it : how to navigate big emotions / Sloane Hughes.
Description: Fusion books. | Minneapolis, Minnesota : Bearport Publishing Company, 2022. | Series: Life works! | Includes index.
Identifiers: LCCN 2021034178 (print) | LCCN 2021034179 (ebook) | ISBN 9781636914268 (library binding) | ISBN 9781636914312 (paperback) | ISBN 9781636914367 (ebook)
Subjects: LCSH: Emotions in children--Juvenile literature. | Emotions--Juvenile literature.
Classification: LCC BF723.E6 H84 2022 (print) | LCC BF723.E6 (ebook) | DDC 155.4/124--dc23
LC record available at https://lccn.loc.gov/2021034178
LC ebook record available at https://lccn.loc.gov/2021034179

Copyright © 2022 Bearport Publishing Company. All rights reserved. No part of this publication may be reproduced in whole or in part, stored in any retrieval system, or transmitted in any form or by any means, electronic, mechanical, photocopying, recording, or otherwise, without written permission from the publisher.

For more information, write to Bearport Publishing, 5357 Penn Avenue South, Minneapolis, MN 55419. Printed in the United States of America.

CONTENTS

When Things Get Big............. 4
Feeling It 6
Our Bodies Talk.................... 8
Checking In 10
From Big to Small................. 12
Pressing Pause 14
A Helping Hand 16
Asking............................ 18
Thinking of Others 20
Why Worry? 22
Glossary.......................... 24
Index 24

WHEN THINGS GET BIG

We all have many feelings every day. Sometimes, they can get really big. It can seem like a feeling takes over everything else.

FEELING IT

Sometimes, emotions make our heads or hearts feel things. Other times, they show up in the rest of our bodies.

OUR BODIES TALK

Our bodies talk to us all the time. And our feelings are part of the chat. What do they say?

What might having red cheeks say? It could mean we are angry or **embarrassed**.

CHECKING IN

Listening to our bodies helps us know when feelings are taking over. Then, we can pick out our emotions.

TRY IT: COLORFUL CHECK-IN

1. Listen to your body. How are you feeling?
2. Pick a color that makes you think of that feeling.
3. Look around and find something the color of your feeling.
4. Are you feeling anything else? Pick a new color and start over!

FROM BIG TO SMALL

Once we know how we feel, what's next? Sometimes, it can be easy to make a big feeling smaller.

But when big feelings won't budge, it might be time to take a break. Doing something else can help. We can **focus** on something other than our big feeling.

Sometimes, walking away from what is giving us big feelings can help.

PRESSING PAUSE

When we need to press pause on big emotions, we can try **meditating**. It is as easy as breathing!

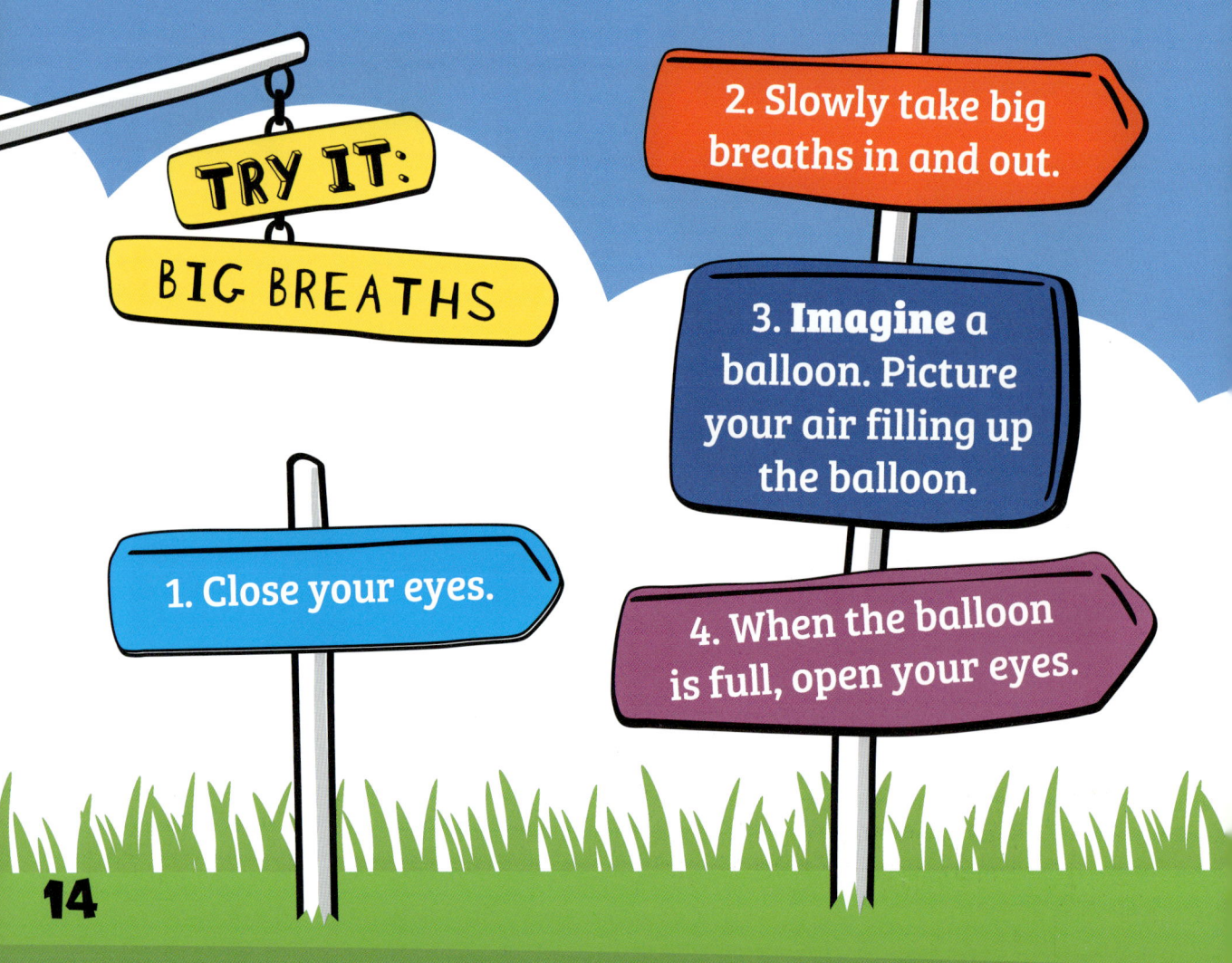

TRY IT: BIG BREATHS

1. Close your eyes.
2. Slowly take big breaths in and out.
3. **Imagine** a balloon. Picture your air filling up the balloon.
4. When the balloon is full, open your eyes.

A HELPING HAND

We may need help to make our big feelings smaller. Asking for help makes us all stronger.

Who is your best helper?

Is there someone to talk to in your family?

Your teacher may be a good listener.

Telling a helper how we're feeling can be a good first step. We can talk to grown-ups who we **trust**.

THINKING OF OTHERS

We all have big feelings. Sometimes, we can be helpers for others with big emotions. When we put ourselves in their shoes, it's called **empathy**.

How does empathy work?

How did it feel?

We think about when we went through something similar.

Then, we imagine how someone else feels.

20

WHY WORRY?

Emotions can be big. But if we listen to our bodies, we can learn how to make them smaller.

Emotions are okay!

GLOSSARY

embarrassed feeling confused or silly in front of others

emotions strong feelings, such as love, anger, joy, or fear

empathy the understanding and sharing of the emotions and feelings of another

focus to give your full attention to something

imagine to picture something in your mind

meditating sitting quietly while focusing on your body and thoughts

nervous worried or afraid of what might happen

trust to believe in someone or something

INDEX

balloon 14
body 7, 10, 23
break 13
breathing 14
check-in 10
emotions 5–6, 10, 14, 18, 20, 22
empathy 20–21
focus 13
helper 16–17, 20
meditating 14